GARFIELD
on the Farm

Created by Jim Davis
Story by Jim Kraft
Illustrated by Mike Fentz

A Golden Book • New York
Western Publishing Company, Inc., Racine, Wisconsin 53404

MCMXC

Jon's family lived on a farm.
Jon took Garfield and Odie there.
"You will like my family," said Jon.
"You will like the farm."
"We will see," said Garfield.

Garfield met Jon's mother and father.
He met Doc Boy.
Doc Boy is Jon's brother.

"You must be hungry
from your trip,"
said Jon's mother.
"Here is a snack."
"I like your mother,"
said Garfield.

They had a big dinner.
Then they sat on the porch.
"Your cat is fat,"
said Doc Boy.
"He is too fat for a cat."

"He is too fat for an elephant,"
said Jon.
"He needs to work,"
said Jon's father.
Garfield did not like to hear that!

"Get up!" said Jon's father
the next day.
"We have work to do."
"I have sleep to do,"
said Garfield.

"Everyone on the farm
has a job," said Jon.
"My mother cooks and cleans.

"My father plows the fields.

"My brother milks the cows.
And I must feed them.

"Odie will watch the sheep,"
said Jon.
"Garfield, you will..."

But Garfield ran!
"I do not want to work,"
he said.
"I must hide!"

Garfield hid in the pigpen.
"Are you a pig?" one pig asked.
"Only at dinnertime,"
answered Garfield.

"This is better than working,"
Garfield thought.
But still it was not fun.

"What do pigs do for fun?"
asked Garfield.
"We throw mud!"
said a pig.
That was not for Garfield.

Garfield ran to the hen house.
"I am safe here," he said.
"And I like this nest."

Garfield hatched an egg!
"Mother?" asked the chick.
"Cat," answered Garfield.

The mother hen saw Garfield
with her baby.
Garfield ran to the barn.

Garfield hid in the barn.
He hid under the hay.

Then Doc Boy came into the barn.

He began to pitch hay.

His pitchfork was sharp.

"Ouch!" cried Garfield.

"I can not hide here.

"I will hide in the cornfield,"
said Garfield.
He tried to climb the fence.
"Help!" cried Garfield.

A goat helped Garfield
over the fence.

"I am sore," said Garfield.
"And I am hungry.
I am tired of hiding.
I will find Jon."

"I give up," said Garfield.
"Hiding from work is
too much work.
Give me a job."

"Hello, Garfield," said Jon.
"You did a good job today."
"I did?" said Garfield.
"Yes," said Jon.
"You did not get in the way.
That was your job.
You did it very well."
"I knew that," said Garfield.

31

At dinner Doc Boy said,
"You eat too much, Garfield."
"Everyone has a job,"
said Garfield.
"My job is to eat!"
And Garfield did that job
very, very well.